BAGDASARIAN
PRODUCTIONS

ALVINNN!!!
AND THE CHIPMUNKS™

Alvin's New Friend

based on the screenplay "Warbie"
written by Janice Karman
adapted by Lauren Forte

Ready-to-Read

Simon Spotlight

New York   London   Toronto   Sydney   New Delhi

SIMON SPOTLIGHT

An imprint of Simon & Schuster Children's Publishing Division
1230 Avenue of the Americas, New York, New York 10020
This Simon Spotlight edition December 2017
Alvin and The Chipmunks, The Chipettes and Characters TM & © 2017 Bagdasarian
Productions, LLC. All Rights Reserved. Agent: PGS USA.

For information about special discounts for bulk purchases, please contact
Simon & Schuster Special Sales at 1-866-506-1949 or business@simonandschuster.com.
Manufactured in the United States of America 1117 LAK
10 9 8 7 6 5 4 3 2 1
ISBN 978-1-5344-0929-3 (hc)
ISBN 978-1-5344-0928-6 (pbk)
ISBN 978-1-5344-0930-9 (eBook)

One sunny afternoon
the Chipmunks and Chipettes
were playing basketball.

Eleanor made a great leaping shot.
It swished through the net,
bonked Theodore on the head,
and bounced into the bushes.

When they ran to get the ball,
they heard a chirping sound
behind the branches.
They all took a peek.

"It's a baby bird," cooed Eleanor.
"I wonder where his momma is,"
Jeanette said. "I'll get a towel
to make him comfortable."

They rested the little bird on the
towel and went inside to
watch what would happen.
They watched . . . and waited.

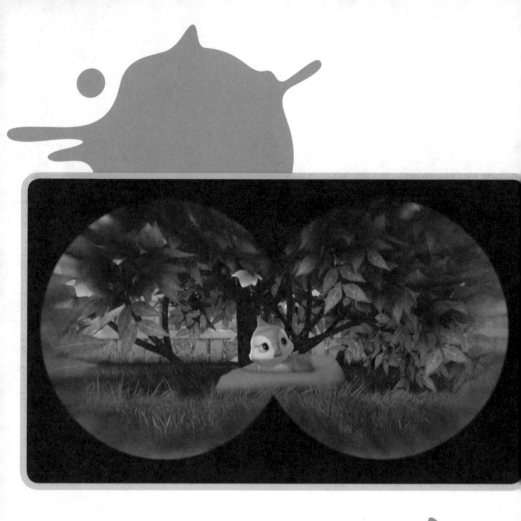

"It's been five hours, guys,"
Simon began. "There's no sign
of his mom."
So they brought the little bird
inside the boys' house.

"We have everything we need," said Simon.

"Yes," confirmed Brittany.

"You guys will be okay caring for him?" asked Eleanor.

Simon laughed. "I think the three of us—"

"Two," Alvin interrupted. "I don't love birds. Especially little ones that need lots of help and attention."

The Chipmunks and Chipettes glared at Alvin but then helped get the baby bird ready for bed.
The girls went home for the night.
The baby bird looked scared.

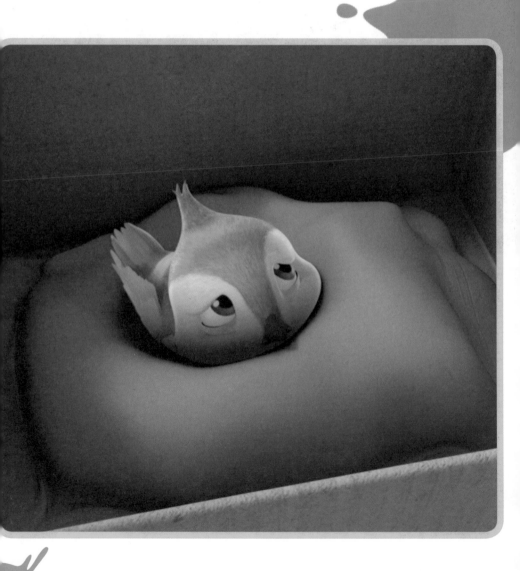

"This is my very special blanket,"
murmured Theodore quietly
as he tucked the bird in.

Eventually, everyone went to sleep.
But in the middle of the night,
Alvin woke up when the bird
started chirping.

"Guys! Wake up!" Alvin called.

But they didn't move.

Alvin peeked in the box at the bird.

"Ugh, are you hungry?

All right. Fine!"

He picked him up.

"Slow down. A little at a time,"
Alvin said, holding the food dropper.
The bird chirped.
"Yeah, yeah. You're welcome,"
Alvin answered.

The next day the girls came over to feed the bird. But he wouldn't eat! "Come on, Warbie," called Alvin. "That's his name?" Brittany asked. "Yes. Alvin named him after a video game," Eleanor explained.

"I got you your own worm,"
Alvin said lovingly.
Warbie ate it right up.
Everyone stared at Alvin.
They were amazed to see that
Alvin liked birds after all.

Two weeks later Dave came
into the kitchen and asked,
"How is Warbie doing today?"
"I'll tell you!" Simon blurted out.
"He has barely left Alvin's sight,
and if Alvin leaves, Warbie
screams till he comes back."

"He sleeps in the bed with him," Simon continued.

"He goes to the bathroom with him. They are too attached to each other."

Later Simon told Alvin
how he was feeling.
"He needs to learn a little
independence," Simon explained.
"Giving in to him is not good."

"Why not?" Alvin responded.

"He's a wild bird," answered Simon.

"He has to learn how to find food and water and how to protect himself."

Alvin decided to try to teach
Warbie himself.
Alvin put on a bird costume
and dug for worms.

Alvin showed him the sink.
Warbie did not move to get water.

"If a bird tries to steal your food,
BAM! Give them a karate chop."
Warbie just stared.

Alvin tried to get him to play with
other birds, but he refused.

Finally, Alvin let Warbie out to play
and closed the door.
But Warbie stayed by the door and
wouldn't move without Alvin.
Nothing was working.

Feeling defeated,
Alvin stared at his food.
Suddenly, the toaster started smoking.
The bread was burning!
Then the smoke alarm went off.

The noise startled Warbie
and he freaked!
He flew all over the house.
"Warbie, stop! Stop!" Alvin cried,
trying to catch him.

But Warbie was in such a panic from
the noise, he didn't realize the window
was closed. He flew into the glass!

"He's hurt!" yelled Simon
as Alvin cradled him in his hands.
"I'll call a doctor!" Theodore said.
The boys were a team again.

The veterinarian arrived quickly
and took Warbie to
the animal hospital.

Alvin was so upset.
Warbie just had to be okay!

A few days passed.
One afternoon the boys came home
from school to find the vet in the yard.
"I found Warbie's nest," she said.
"He is doing great. His mom will
look after him now."
Just then Warbie flew down and
landed on Alvin's hand.

"My buddy!" Alvin cooed.
"Remember, if it's too crowded
in the nest, you can always sleep over."
They were best friends forever!